lauren child

I've won, NO I'VE WON, No I've won

Grosset & Dunlap

Charlie and Lola™

Text based on script written by Dave Ingham

Illustrations from the TV animation produced by Tiger Aspect

GROSSET & DUNLAP
Published by the Penguin Group
Penguin Group (USA) Inc., 375 Hudson Street, New York, New York 10014, U.S.A.
Penguin Group (Canada), 90 Eglinton Avenue East, Suite 700, Toronto, Ontario, Canada M4P 2Y3
(a division of Pearson Penguin Canada Inc.)
Penguin Books Ltd, 80 Strand, London WC2R 0RL, England
Penguin Ireland, 25 St Stephen's Green, Dublin 2, Ireland
(a division of Penguin Books Ltd)
Penguin Group (Australia), 250 Camberwell Road, Camberwell, Victoria 3124, Australia
(a division of Pearson Australia Group Pty Ltd)
Penguin Books India Pvt Ltd, 11 Community Centre, Panchsheel Park, New Delhi - 110 017, India
Penguin Group (NZ), Cnr Airborne and Rosedale Roads, Albany, Auckland 1310, New Zealand
(a division of Pearson New Zealand Ltd)
Penguin Books (South Africa) (Pty) Ltd, 24 Sturdee Avenue, Rosebank, Johannesburg 2196, South Africa

Penguin Books Ltd, Registered Offices:
80 Strand, London WC2R 0RL, England

First published in Great Britain 2005 by Puffin Books.
Text and illustrations copyright © Lauren Child/Tiger Aspect Productions Limited, 2006
The Charlie and Lola logo is a trademark of Lauren Child. All rights reserved.
First published in the United States 2006 by Grosset & Dunlap, a division of Penguin Young Readers Group, 345 Hudson Street, New York, New York 10014. GROSSET & DUNLAP is a trademark of Penguin Group (USA) Inc. Manufactured in China.

ISBN 978-0-448-44350-8   10 9 8 7 6 5 4 3

I have this little sister, Lola.
        She is small and very funny.
        Sometimes we play "Who can sit
still the longest!"
        Lola **always** has to win.

Last time we played, Lola said, "I've won!"

I say,
"But I didn't even move!"

Lola says,
"Yes you did! I've won!
I always win . . .
always,
always,
always!"

And then she says,

"I could even beat a speedy, speedy cheetah in a running race, and I can stand on one leg longer than a flamingo!

And I can bounce higher than a bouncy **kangaroo**, Charlie! See!

And I can **drink** my pink milk
much **faster** than you."
I say,
"But do you have to **win** at **everything**, Lola?"

And Lola says,

"Yep. I've won!"

So I say,
"How about a game
of spoons?"

Because, you see,
I know I'm better
at the spoon game.

But even so,
Lola says, "I'm winning!"
I say, "No you're not!"
She says, "I am."
I say, "Not!"

And then Lola
says,
"Ooh, Charlie,
what's that?"

I look off to
the side
and then when
I look back
at Lola . . .

her spoon has **definitely** moved!
I say,
"Lola, have you... **cheated?**"
But Lola says,
"Charlie, **I've won!**"

So then I say,
"Lola, you remember how to play **snap**,
don't you?
You need **two cards** that look the **same**,
then it's a **snap**."

Lola says,
"Yes, **two cards** that look
exactly the **same**,
then it's a
snap."

So I say,
"**five**."

So then I say,
"How about a game of **snakes and ladders?**
You go
up the **ladders**
and
down the **snakes!**
The one who gets to
the **top** first is the **winner!**
Do you understand?"

Lola says, "I **do** understand, yes, Charlie!"

I roll first and I shout...

"Six!

1 . . 2 . . 3 . . 4 . . 5 . . 6

and

up

the

ladder!"

Then it's Lola's turn and she shouts . . .
      "That's a **three! Snake!**"

            I say,
"Lola, what are you doing?
      Snakes are for sliding **down**.
It's the rules!"
Lola says,
"But Charlie, everyone knows snakes aren't all slippy and slidy.

They're

easy

to climb.

And . . .

I'm winning!'

Luckily I get another **six**, which means **up** a **ladder!**

But Lola says,

"Aha! Dad said you are not allowed to **climb** a **ladder!** Not until you are **twenty-three!**"

I say,

"Uh-huh. **Up** the **ladders** and **down** the **snakes.** **That's the rules!**"

So Lola shakes the dice and says, "four! 1....2....3....4 snake!"

I say, "Bad luck. Now you've got to slide down all the way to the bottom. I've won!"

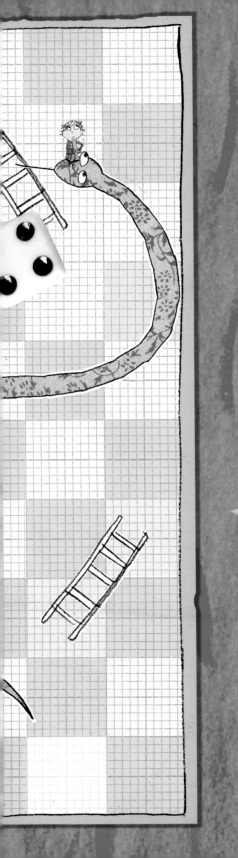

But guess what?
Lola pretends she's a **snake** charmer

and she charms the snake to the finish.

I say,
"But that's
cheating, Lola."

And she says,

"**No, I've won!**"

So I think of something
that Lola could
        never, never **win**!

When we go to the park
        I say,
"How about a **race**?
            It's **once** round
        the **bendy tree**!
Then **two** big swings
        on the **swing**!
Down the slide . . .
        and **first** one back
to the **bench**
        is
            the
            winner! Okay?"

Lola says,
"But I'm only little, Charlie.
        I haven't been on the big slide yet."

        And I say,
        "Well if you don't want
                to win the race, Lola . . ."

And guess what? I'm actually winning!

"And that's two big swings on the swing!"

But then Lola calls,
"Charlie!
Can
you
help
me?"

And even though
          I'm actually winning,
     I say,
"All right, Lola,
     I'm coming!
          Hold on."

We w h o o s h

down

the slide

together.

Lola says,

"Wheeeee-eeee!
I'm winning!"

I say,

Then I say,
"And the
winner is . . .

me!

"Not for long!"

I've
won!
I've won!"

Then I remember Dad saying,
"Charlie, you must give Lola a chance,
because she's so **small** . . ."

And I say,
"Are you all right, Lola?"

And do you know what Lola says?
She says,

"That was fun!"

And I say,
"Even though
I won . . . ?"

Lola says,
"Charlie, you don't
**have to win
all the time,**
you know!"

At bedtime, I say,
"Are you **asleep**
       yet, Lola?"

And Lola says,
    "Yes."

    So I say,
"How can you be **asleep**
if you are **talking** to me?"

She says,
    "I'm **sleep-talking!**"

    I say,
"The **first one** to
       fall **asleep** is
the **real winner!**"

And Lola says,
    "Okay. The **first one**
to fall **asleep** is
    the **real winner.**"

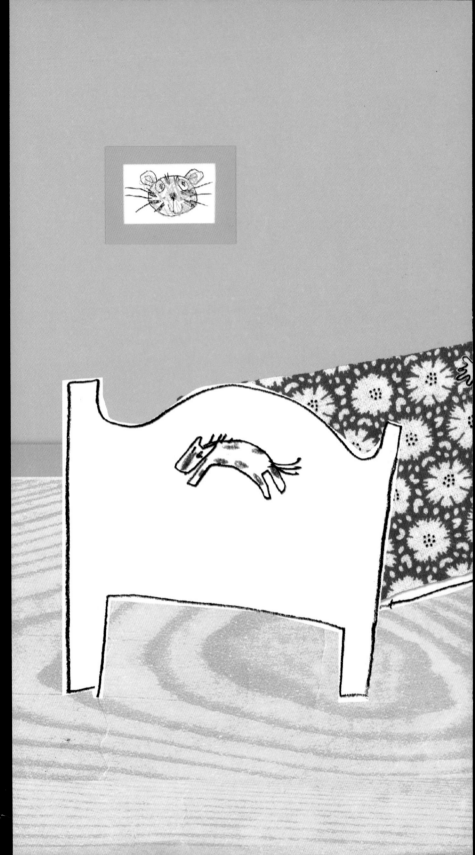

And then Lola whispers, "Charlie? I've won!"
And I say, "No . . . I've won!"
"I've won!"
"No . . . I've won!"
"I've won!"